Thomas and the Green Controller

Based on *The Railway Series* **by The Rev. W. Awdry**

First published in Great Britain 2008 by Egmont UK Limited

239 Kensington High Street, London W8 6SA

Thomas the Tank Engine & Friends™

CREATED BY BRITT ALLCROFT

Based on The Railway Series by The Reverend W Awdry
Photographs © 2008 Gullane (Thomas) LLC. A HiT Entertainment Company

HiT entertainment

Thomas the Tank Engine & Friends and Thomas & Friends are trademarks of Gullane (Thomas) Limited.
Thomas the Tank Engine & Friends and Design is Reg. US. Pat. & Tm. Off.

ISBN 978 1 4052 3866 3

1 3 5 7 9 10 8 6 4 2

Printed in China

It was a quiet day at Tidmouth Sheds. Percy was all alone.

Suddenly, The Fat Controller's car pulled up. Percy was very surprised when Lady Hatt and her friends got out of the car instead!

"Sir Topham is sick," she announced, grandly. "He has lost his voice."

Percy was worried. "I hope he finds it soon," he peeped.

Lady Hatt read out a list of jobs from The Fat Controller. "Gordon is to collect coaches of china from Knapford and take them to the Docks ... he must go very slowly."

"Slow cars," peeped Percy.

"James is to shunt trucks in the Coal Yards ... he must be as busy as a bee," Lady Hatt went on.
"Busy bee!" puffed Percy.

"And Toby is to take visitors to the Scottish Castle ... he must go as fast as Gordon's Express!"
"Gordon's Express," puffed Percy.

"You're in charge now, Percy," said Lady Hatt.

Just then, Thomas puffed in from his morning's work.

"I'm Controller for the day," peeped Percy, proudly.

"Do you need any help?" Thomas asked his friend.

"Controllers don't need help!" wheeshed Percy.

And off he chuffed.

Percy found Gordon first. "The Fat Controller has lost his voice," puffed Percy. "So I am Controller until he finds it!"

Gordon was surprised.

Percy tried hard to remember what Lady Hatt had said. "You must pull very slow cars!" he peeped.

"Oh, the indignity!" huffed Gordon.

Percy had a lot to do and a lot to remember!

Next, Percy found James at the Washdown.

"James, you must be a busy bee!" he peeped.

James gasped. "Do you mean I have to be yellow and black?" he whistled.

"Yes, James," Percy said, sternly.
James was angry. He wanted to keep his red paint!

"I am Controller! Engines must do as they are told," Percy boomed, as he puffed away.

Next, Percy found Toby. "Toby, you must pull Gordon's Express!" he told him.

"Why?" Toby asked. He was very puzzled.

"That's your job," peeped Percy, loudly.

Percy felt very important.

Later, Percy decided it was time to check on his engines.

He knew that's what The Fat Controller would do.

Some children were waiting on the bridge.
Percy peeped, "hello".

But the children were looking at the track where
Gordon was puffing slowly down the line.

The children began to laugh. "Look at Gordon,"
they cried, "what a slowcoach!"

Then James stopped at the signal. The children laughed again.

James' splendid red paintwork was not splendid or red any more – he had been painted with yellow and black stripes.

"Who is that giant stripy bee?" the children called.

Finally, Toby the Tram Engine huffed in with the heavy Express.

It was very hard work for a little engine like him, and Toby was tired.

"My axles ache!" poor Toby wheeshed to James.

Gordon, James and Toby heard the children laughing. And they saw Percy watching.

Gordon called out to Percy, "I am supposed to be the fastest engine on Sodor! Not the slowest!" he huffed.

"I'm supposed to be the reddest engine," moaned James. "Now no one knows who I am!"

"I'm only a steam tram," Toby puffed. "The Express is too heavy for me to pull."

Percy was worried. He knew he had made lots of mistakes.

Then Thomas puffed up. "What's wrong, Percy?" he asked his friend.

"Please help me, Thomas. I can't remember what Lady Hatt told me. All the engines are doing the wrong jobs."

Thomas thought for a moment. "You must go back over your tracks," he puffed. "You might see things that will help you remember."

Percy thought that was a very good idea.

Thomas and Percy pulled into Knapford Station.

"Gordon and slow cars," puffed Percy.

Suddenly, Percy saw crates of china waiting on the platform.

"That's it!" Percy cried. "Gordon is to take the china to the Docks. He must pull his coaches very slowly!"

Percy and Thomas puffed into the Coal Yards.

"James must be a busy bee," Percy said, slowly.

There were lots of grumbling coal trucks waiting to be shunted.

"That's it – James is to shunt lots of trucks! So, he must be as busy as a bee!" smiled Percy.

Finally, Percy and Thomas arrived at the station.

"Toby must pull Gordon's Express," puzzled Percy.

Suddenly, Percy saw a group of visitors, waiting on the platform. "That's it!" he cried. "Toby is to take visitors to the Scottish Castle! He has to go as fast as Gordon's Express!"

Later, The Fat Controller came to the Sheds.

"You have done well, little Percy," he smiled.
"I'm very pleased."

"And I'm very pleased that you've found your voice."
Percy peeped, happily. "I just hope you never lose
it again!"

Did you enjoy the story?
Can you answer these questions?

1) Which engine was put in charge of the Railway?

2) Which engine had to go very slowly?

3) Which engine was as busy as a bee?

4) Which engine helped Percy remember what to do?